Mandarayakshi
The story of six murders
Mysteries of witchcraft and Indian black magic

Horror Novel

Vinod Narayanan

NYNA BOOKS
www.nynabooks.com

English Language
Mandarayakshi
(Novel)
Vinod Narayanan
Rights Reserved

First Malayalam print Edition: November 2019
First English print Edition: June 2022

Cover & Typesetting: Boons Entertainments

Published by
NYNA BOOKS
MSME/UAN Regd. KL07D0004957
www.nynabooks.com
Email: nynabooks@gmail.com

ISBN: 9798838380807

Vinod Narayanan

Vinod Narayanan is an Indian author. He was born on March 24, 1975 at Thripunithura in Ernakulam district, Kerala state in India. His father Chottanikkara Velumbarambil Naraya nan and his mother Thrippunithura Eroor Vaniyathuparambil Omana. He studied in Chottanikkara Govt Arts College and Thripunithura Govt College. After graduating in history he became a journalist. Now he is an independent writer and screenwriter. Five short films were scripted and screened in various international film Festivals and won awards.

The first novel 'Mayakkottaram' (The Magic Palace) was published in 1999 at Manorajyam weekly. He has published forty short stories in different periodicals. More than 160 books have been published by various publishers. The main books are "The Red" (novel), "Double murder" (Novel), Mandara yakshi (Novel), Mumbai Restaurant (Novel), Nayika (Novel), Kamika (Novel), Welcome to Kochi (Novel) and other Malayalam books. Black night gown (Film script), Incest (Stories), the imagination of secret lover (Stories), Talking birds (Stories) are his English fictions. Also he wrote 60 children's books.

Address:
'Sivaranjani'
Chempu. P.O, PIN: 686608
Vaikom, Kottayam district,
Kerala state, India
Phone: 9567216134
Email: boonsenter@gmail.com

"As long as there is the semen of Kandakattan in her abdomen, Mandarayakshi will not leave her. The semen of the Kandakattan is born as the Keeladwwajan. It is the incarnation of Keelakan, one of the thirty-two Ketu, the sons of Rahu. All the men who try to sex her will be killed. Human men cannot satisfy Mandarayakshi, the fourteenth Vadayakshini, in sex. "

Introduction

A woman's mind is like the sky. It is an endless lake full of stars and black holes. Salome wants to kill her husband. The path she chose for it, however, was fraught with danger. The novel opens the door to the mysteries of witchcraft and Indian black magic. Mandarayakshi, the symbol of the erotic Vadayakshini, is the epitome of sexuality and pleasure. It is a symbol of eyeless lust that embraces death. Apart from being a horror novel, it is also a crime thriller that keeps the suspense in every line.

Chapter 1

Salome sat in a small room with dim lighting.
A ghee lamp was burning in one corner of the table.
The smell of incense lingered throughout the room.
Opposite, the astrologer looked at her through her spectacles. It was clear from the visiting cards stacked in a small box on the table that her name was Lalitha.
The woman in the saffron sari looked about fifty-five years old.
There was an ash thilak on her forehead.
In the corner of the woman's eye, her visitor's reaction was obvious.
Salome was bathed in sweat by panic.
In the zodiac on the table, the planets are holding the position of the planets.
"Let me tell you about your wedding. "
"Tell me, madam. I want to know for myself. "
"Salome, I see a lot of trouble in your future."
Salome was shocked.

Lalitha looked carefully at the zodiac. She has met many like this in their careers. But Salome was more upset than they were.

She looked through the simple zodiac sign again.

"I see only trouble in your future."

"About Sebastian."

"Let me tell you - yes, your husband Sebastian will die. "

Salome looked at Lalitha in shock.

But her gut throbbed.

She wants Sebastian to die as soon as possible.

"Ma'am, I want that. Will Sebastian die soon? "

"Absolutely."

"When ...?"

"I cannot say that now. But you have to work hard. "

"I told you ... he's a fatal patient. Wheelchair user. He is 48 years old which means he is 20 years older than me but he has money. I want that. "

"You have suffered for him for a long time."

"Madame is right. I saw a lot of sadness and grief. My youth is burning. "

"Before the liberation of life comes, sorrow is for your thoughts. If there is no grief, you will not think. "
Lalitha said philosophy.

"How long have I been fascinated by thoughts."
Salome wiped away the tears.
"He will surely die."
"But I do not want him to suffer anymore."
Salome paused and asked, "...can his death be hastened?"
Lalitha leaned back in her chair with a restless mind. When the forehead frowned, the dust fell from the ash thilak. They said in disgust
"I can't do things like this. I can but I will not. I only care about the future. "
"Madam, are you saying this and setting fire to my mind and retreating?"
Salome said sadly.
"I am just telling the truth. Astrology tells us not to tell unpleasant truths. But I do not lie to my clients. Because Lord Murugan says that hiding the truth is like lying. "
"Can't it be done with your Murugan?"

"It is possible. It has been done many times. But not now. I stopped it. "
"Please madam."
Salome begged as if on her feet.
Lalitha spectacles were placed on the table.
"People like you hate people like us after all. Secretly sees things with us and publicly calls it bad. Why can't you live with Sebastian? "
"How...what did I say so much?"
"He will stay at home. Why don't you choose a friend..? "
Lalitha said with ease.
Salome was silent.
She thought. How to tell about Sandeep.
"That ... madam ... with another man while my husband was alive ...?"
She looked into her eyes to see if she had simply believed what she was saying; hiding the fact that she had spent several nights with Sandeep in her large bungalow.
Lalitha smile.
The tail of laugh protruded from the corner of their lips.
Salome is a fool who thought you could lie to a Jolsya like that. "
Salome lowered her head

"To be honest, madam. I cannot live with Sebastian. Get him out of my life. "
"You can leave him easily!"
"But he has huge assets. Acres of land. There is also a large bank balance. Money is not a problem for me. "
"I told you I could not do it."
"All right. If madam does not do that, introduce someone who can. "
"Are you getting up ..?"
Lalitha is upset.
Salome said patiently again
"Madam pleases ..!"
"Please go ... you will come up with a Spy cam and shoot what I say and put it on the channel or YouTube."
Salome immediately opened the bag, took out five thousand rupees currency, and laid them on the table - "Look, madam, no one pays that much for an astrologer." Can a channel person who comes with a spy camera give like this? "

Lalitha look at the currency.
Then she picked it up, put it in the desk drawer and stuck something on a piece of paper.
Then she stretched the piece of paper towards Salome and said gently:

"He can definitely help you."
Salome said goodbye to Lalitha and left.

She lied to Sebastian that there was a cultural program in Kochi. She was told to stay in a hostel with her girlfriend. But she only slept in Sandeep's flat at night. Sandeep did not know that she went to see Lalitaji in the morning. He should not know that. Because these males are a special kind. Doesn't he think that working with Sebastian may not show Sandeep tomorrow? Otherwise, he does not intend to lead Sandeep full time in his life.

Chapter 2

Salome took a taxi to Sandeep's flat in Kundannur near Vyttila.

While in the taxi, she read the address given by Lalitha.

The said person lives in Mutharamala near Pulippara waterfall in Wayanad. It will be convenient to leave for Wayanad now.

If I pack my belongings from Sandeep's flat and take a train from Ernakulam, I can take a bus to Wayanad in the morning.

Salomi calls Sandeep on mobile.

"I'm going to Kozhikode."

"Suddenly ... why don't you come here tonight ..?"

"Not enough. I want to see Alifa. She will be waiting for me in Kozhikode. "

"Okay...go and call...you know where the key to the flat is." "

"Oh right."

She booked a hotel room in Kozhikode through Trevago.

ooooooooo

Salomi got off a KSRTC bus at Vaithiri in Wayanad and took a taxi.
Got it through Uber.
The taxi driver was a short black young man.
Salome asked his name.
He was named Ali.
She showed him the address slip.
After reading it, Ali looked at her skeptically.
"No car will go here, madam.”
“Then the car will go where. .?”
"You can go by car to the Andheri Junction. From there you can get a jeep to Pulippara. Few tourists come there. Then no one goes to Mutharamala. ”
“Why?”
“There are no people there.”
“And how does this man live there?”
“Who is the Uttaswamy mentioned in this?”
“Yes.”
“I did not even hear about him," he said. ”

Salome was not disappointed by the taxi driver's words.

With her travel experience, she realized that the country's knowledge of an Uber taxi driver would be limited. She shared the practical wisdom of being able to go to the place mentioned in the address. If she can rely on Google Maps, then Uthaswamy is not the one who gave the location in Google.

The car moved into the inner lane of Wayanadu. The road was deserted. There was snow in the roadside woods.
While in the backseat, Salome saw driver Ali's eyes fall on her through the rearview mirror. She was holding her right hand in the pepper spray in the bag she regularly carries on trips.

The car reached the Antheery Junction in three and a half hours.
After giving Ali the money, Salome went down the junction.
A jeep with four or five tourists is waiting at the intersection to go to Pulippara Falls. Salome gets into it.
It was eight o'clock in the morning. The sun is slowly clearing. The snow in the atmosphere slowly begins to melt.
The jeep started climbing the hill.

It was extremely difficult to navigate the steep gravel road.
Salome wondered if she would throw away from the jeep for a shake.
In half an hour, the jeep reached the Pulippara waterfall.
It's not a big waterfall.
The snow was beginning to move as the sun's rays got stronger.
Salome, along with other travelers, bathed in the waterfall.
The water was nice and cool.

A few locals are sitting in a nearby tea shop.
Salome went to the store.
She bought a cup of tea.
The tea did not taste great. And the one who gave the tea was ugly.
She asked a local man:
“Do you know Uttaswamy from Mutharamala?”
“Oh, one-eyed Utta ...”
Someone scoffed.
“Hey man, you cannot say that. You will not be in the morning tomorrow. ”
The tea shop owner warned that man.
"Is that such a goon?”
Salome asked nervously

“Do you know anything about him?”
The tea shop owner asked.
“I needed one. This is the address given by an astrologer to see him. That's how I got here. ”
"What's your name?”
“Salome.”
The tea shop owner thought for a second.
“Are you a Christian?”
“Yes.”
“Such witchcraft will be done there ... witchcraft ...”
The last words were said in silence.
"If Utta decides to kill someone by magic, it will happen.”
Salome's chest throbbed when she heard those words.
“Then ... what will he do next?”
She asked anxiously.
“Evil ... gang ... he can destroy a family. He can close a factory, and he can easily divide two people. ”
Salome wanted to see him as soon as possible.
Salome regained her composure when she realized that she had come to the right place.
“Will you show me his house ...?”

Salome said.
The tea shop owner looked around.
"Whoever comes with me may have a fee... sure."
When Salome said that, agreed that a middle-aged man with spring-like hair would come.
"Chintan will come with you ...he is a forest dweller...he knows the forest well ..."
Salome paid a hundred rupees to the tea shop owner who gave her so much valuable information.
She walked with Chintan.

Chapter 3

The steep climb along the edge of the waterfall is full of rocks. All I can say is that there is a sidewalk. Salome had a hard time keeping up with Chintan.
Chintan did not speak much.
When she was worried about walking, Salome, who was far behind, called out:
"Hey Chintan...stay there ..."
He turned and stood.
"I am just happy to be free."
Salome opened the bag and drank the water.

She gestured to him if he needed water.
He shakes the shoulder, meaning no.

Then their walk continued.
Forest path.
An uninhabited place.
Occasionally saw hot shit of elephants.
The sound of an elephant's call was heard somewhere nearby.
Salome was frightened.
She ran and started walking after Chintan.

"Is there a leopard here, Chinda?"
Salome tried to active the man who was walking silently.
"Um ...Tiger...Bear...Elephant ..."
Chintan said.
"Why does this Uttaswamy come and live in this forest?"
"I don't know ... He will be able to do penance."
Salome struggled to keep up with the fast-moving Chintan.

At the end of the trek, they crossed the grassy valley and reached Mutharamala.
A mountain that sits like the curved beak of a bird.
A hut clinging to it.
"That is Swami's hut."
Chintan pointed out.
"Iso...how can I climb?"
Salome asked excitedly.
Chintan began to tread on the rocks that lay upwards like pebbles.
Salome followed him.

After some effort, they reached the top of the Muthara hill.

Ottakannan Uthaswamy's hut on top of the hill.
A terrible dog was sitting on the porch of the hut.
When it saw them, it began to growl terribly.
Salome and Chintan were scared.
It jumped out off the floor.
Salome and Chintan stepped back in fear.
She decided to go back and run.
"Anoop ...!"
Someone called from inside.
The dog's bark softened a little.
"Who is ...?"
A man came out from inside.

An old man in a black robe with a red knot on top of it and another red knot on his shoulder. Healthy man. He has only one eye. Only a lump of flesh in the position of the right eye.
"Anoop ... shut up ..."
He told the dog.
The dog's name is Anoop. I do not know if anyone can name a dog Anoop.
Salome laughed when she saw Anoop staring at me, leaning back on the mat.
"How are you ...... is Anoop super?"

He asked seriously.
"I'm scared."
Salome said
"This Anoop has a secret."
Then he asked Chintan.
"Who is this ...?"
"She came to the junction and told me to see Swami ..."
"Didn't I tell you not to cross this forest...why are you bringing all those who saw you here ..?"
The old man nodded angrily.

All of Salome's strength faded.
She looked at Chintan.
"Don't see you here ... you go ..."
The old man said mercilessly to Chintan.
Chintan looked at Salome miserably and began to back away.
Then Salome turned away.
"Where are you going?"
The voice of the old man.
"No ... I ..."
Salome worried.
"Why did you come ...?"
The old man looked down at her.

He licked her body with one eye, wrapped in a white kurta and blue jeans.

"You're not right."
Salome lowered her eyes, unable to meet his eyes.
"I know what you mean ... but you have to hear it from your mouth ... come on."
He invited her into the hut.

Salome looked down at Chintan.
Poor thing. I want to give him some money.
Salome calls Chintan:
"Hey ..."
"Why are you calling him ... let him go."
"I want to give him some money."
"Why ... don't give that dog any money."
What a wicked man.
Salome thought to herself.
"You are the evil."
He said aloud.
Salome was shocked.
"Um...come in ..."
He went inside.
Salome took off her shoes and climbed onto the floor.
Anoop, the dog, did not mind her.

Chapter 4

The floor in the inner room was lined with a mat made of grass.
Dung waxy floor.
Wall covered with wood planks and palm fronds.
The prayer room is different.
He lay down; cooking and eating are all in the main room.
There is a fireplace in the corner.

The old man is sitting on a wood plank.
Salome sat on the grass mat.
"Speak with your mouth. Do you not intend to kill your husband? "
Salome was shocked. How did the old man know this?
Then she calmed down. Jotsya Lalitha should be his agent. He got the information from Lalitha. She must have phoned and said.
"Who sent you to see Uthaswamy?"
"Lalitha."
"Which Lalitha...will Lalitha say anything, will you come up here ..?"

The old man is acting. He does not know how to treat women. If I complain to the Women's Commission, he will go to jail.
"Do you have a camera?"
He asked unexpectedly.
"What?"
Salome asked in shock, unaware.
"Do you have a hidden camera ...?"
"No, Swami ... I'm not really a journalist ... I can give you any amount of money."
"Isn't that your dying money? I don't want that. Or why should I be doing penance in the jungle?" I live without money. Can you live without money for an hour? "
Salome nodded, unable to face that zealous one-eyed man.

As he looks, my nipples tighten and some comfortable muscles under the abdomen twitch.
He was staring at her.
Salome said:
"My husband is a terminally ill patient. Currently wheelchair accessible only. He's 48 years old ... I'm only 28 years old. "
"Didn't the family forcibly tie you up after seeing his money?"

"Yes. But I love him. "
"You will kill him out of love, don't you?"
"I remember his suffering. Why live in this comfortable world without being able to experience it? Wouldn't it be better to die? "
"But you do not avoid your obstacles."
"He's still not a hindrance to me. I have a boyfriend. I can accomplish my things. "

"Do you mean the euthanasia of a husband out of sympathy?"
"Yes."
"What ways do you have for that?"
"Which way?"
"You can mix cyanide in food and finish him in a minute. Many are doing it now. Or you could be strangled him to death and hanged. He can fall head over heels in the bathroom. Suppose he fell and hit his head and died. How easy it is to make it all look like a natural death. "
"I do not want to commit murder."
Salome expressed helplessness.
"Then what do you say I should do?"
Uthaswamy looked at her mysteriously.
"Some kind of black magic act or Koodothram ... I do not know what that thing is ... the person must disappear.

Let no one know that I am behind it. A completely natural death ... then..! "
She stopped in her tracks.
"Then ...?"
"I need to get sympathy for it. I should be respected as a poor widow and people should be kind to me. The property must be secured in such a way that not even an heir is entangled. "
Salome was careful to list her needs meticulously.

Uthaswamy engaged in deliberation.
"I will give you as much money as you want."
Salome said.
On hearing this, Uttaswamy uttered a bad word.
"The money ... money ... That puts in your pussy...."
Salome was shocked at his sudden change of expression.
He moaned angrily
"Didn't I tell you earlier ... I don't want money ... I don't need money to live on this earth."
"Then what do you want. Swami should help me. "

Salome wept and knelt before him.
Uthaswamy's anger subsided.
He said after a few seconds
"We have to do a pooja tonight. You can leave tomorrow morning. "
Salome looked around and wondered how she could spend a night here.
"It is a pooja in which you are also involved. The Moorthy you want to please will come face to face. "
"I am scared, Swami."
"Why should you be afraid? I'm here. I control all these Moorthese. I am a worshiper of the Karna Pishachini. I can know what you have in mind and what your husband's brother Williams in California has in mind. "

Salome was shocked to hear Uttaswamy speak.
Williams, California. I had just heard that Sebastian had such a brother. How did Swami know this?
Salome's eyes filled with devotion. The lips parted.
"Swami ..."
Salome touched Swami's black feet.

Swami said:

"If you are hungry, there is rice in the pot and curd in the pan. There is salt in the salt bottle and chili in the outside yard. "
Salome complied.

She went to the back of the hut. There is a well.
It has good depth. She drew water from a bucket of water. Nice cold. Wash face with water. Then she plucked the chilies from the back yard and washed a flat pan and brought it to the kitchen. She was eaten with rice, yogurt, salt, and chili.
And it tasted good when I drank cold natural water.
Uthaswamy is preparing for the pooja.
By then it was noon.
The mobile did not seem particularly useful as there was no range on the mobile.

Chapter 5

Salome stood on top of Mutharamala and spent time looking at the valley and the forest. She saw the sunset over the western woods.

When it got dark, Utha Swami took a bath from the side of the well and went into the prayer room wearing red silk.
He said before
"We have to wait for three hours."
Salome spent time in the living room and dining room.
Anoop was on guard in Varanta.
He never looked at her.
The moon was rising.
The valley bathed in moonlight.
Various sounds were heard from the forest as a sign that the nightingales and nocturnal animals were waking up and moving.
Salome looked at her watch
It's going to be eleven at night.
The time Swami had said was over.
She looked impatiently at the door of the prayer room.

It was reopened half an hour later.
Swami came out.
The smell of agarbathies wafted out.
Swami had a mixed smell of gorochanam and gopichandanam.
Salome felt as if she were standing near some source of power.
"You take a bath."
Swami took red silk and gives her.
"You need to wear this ... only this."
A command power in Swami's voice.
Salome unknowingly reached out and grabbed the red silk.

She went to the side of the well and took off her jeans, kurta, and underwear, and hung them on a tree branch.
Now she is completely naked.

She looked around. Moonlight laughs and hugs Mutharamala.
She drew cold water and poured it over her head.
Not even a towel to wipe the head. She wiped the water off her head with her kurta and put on red silk. It was only big enough to cover the breasts and barely the thighs. She went inside.

When he knocked on the door of the prayer room, it opened.

Swami invited her inside.

"Come on."

Salome entered the prayer room.

The room was decorated with lights.

In the middle of the room, broomstick lights are lit and stabbed on a decorative Kalam made of Vasha Pindi. On one side she can see the statue of Kandakattan. In front of the idol are two large vessels filled with red and black water of blood color called Guruthy. Swami pointed to a pedestal decorated for her.

"Sit there."

Salome sat on the red silk pedestal.

She felt embarrassed because the silk she was wearing did not cover her body properly.

"Do not hesitate ... why to be ashamed in front of Kandakakattan Swami   ... let your thing happen."

Uttaswamy said.

Salome sat on the pedestal.

The little silk never covered her thighs and waist.

"Kandakakattan Swami is going to fulfill your need. It will happen if Swami decides."

Salome's heart began to throb.
Uttaswami touched the ashes on her forehead.
With that, Salome's consciousness plunged into a magical circle.
Salome's mind began to fly to a level of intoxication.

Uttaswamy gave her theertham in a jug.
It was vodka.
Salome bought it and drank it.
She felt like her throat was burning.
"This is an offering to Kandakakattaswamy. Swami has Panchamakaradi poojas. Mantra, Mudra, Alcohol, Meat, and Sex are the Panchamakara Puja. "
Utta Swami said so and gave her a piece of fried chicken to eat. Salome was in a special state of insanity.
Swami showered flowers on her body.
"Now you are Mandarayakshiamma. I am only a worshiper. "
Fear had left Salome's mind.
Now she felt like she was someone else.
She has tremendous strength and confidence.
She was all shaken up.

The silk she was wearing was removed and her genitals were exposed.
Utta Swami offered flowers there.
"This is Yoni Puja."
Then she felt something strong energy flowing from under her abdomen. In Murdha, the energy above the Sahasrara Padma rushed to the Kundalini below through the Sushunmanadi with the power of a thousand elephants.
The petals of the vagina spread and tremble.
Salome's lips parted.
And nipples.
She got up on some impulse and stood on the pedestal dancing.
The silk came loose from her body.

Chapter 6

Salome's perfectly naked body shone in the light of the lamps.
Uttaswamy chanted mantras and the flower was thrown on her body.

Salome began to dance, displaying her sexual conduct.
Utta Swamy hugs her:
"Mother, I am allowing Kandakakattaswamy to enter me."
Sitting on the Padmasana on the Uthaswamy Peetha, he clasped both his hands and chanted the mantra intensely.
Salome continued to dance.

Uthaswamy's body shook at the height of the mantra.
Kandakakattaswamy has entered him.
Swami jumped up and down.

Swami, who is completely naked, is not old enough to be affected by old age now. He is a Kandakakattaswamy with an iron body. The power of the quoted

Shiva form of the penis shook the atmosphere.

The red blood and the black blood, which were filled in large frying pans, were picked up with both hands and drained.

It was impossible for ordinary people. Then he drank alcohol and ate meat. He looked at Salome dancing on the pedestal.

It was a beautiful Mandarayakshi.
Mandarayakshi with broad thighs like a banana tree and breasts like nectar jars.
Mandarayakshi is the fourteenth of the Vadayakshinis.
She cannot be satisfied with sex with humans. If sex is not satisfied with her, Mandarayakshi's method is to split the man's breast and drink blood from the heart.
Swami approached her.
Both of them danced happily.
They roared like cobras.
At the end of the dance, Swami entered her.
A meeting of two forces.
Rare moments when Mandara Yakshi and Kandakakataswamy matc.

The atmosphere was muffled and witnessed.
It all came together just before the end of time.

ooooooooo

At dawn, Salome opened her eyes.
She was lying completely naked on the floor of the prayer room.
The morning sun seeps in through the cracks in the wall.
The flickering lights all around. Pooja vessels.
Pain as if the body had been crushed.

She tried to remember what had happened that night.
She could feel the sex fluids drying up in her genitals.
Swami raped me.
She was angry.

Salome took and wears the silk lying on the floor and opened the door of the prayer room and went out
Utta Swamy was sitting on the doorstep and smoking a beedi.

“You were cheating on me, weren't you?
You are a liar. " ”
Salome sighed loudly.
Uthaswamy slowly turned around.
“Who one cheated on you. But I ... how
did I cheat.
“You cheated me ...?”
“I did nothing to you.”
“Then ...?"
"It is Kandakakattaswamy ... Swami has
sexed with Mandarayakshi. But not you.
You do not even have the guts to hold
Swami's breathe. Then how do you feel
the Shiva lingam... ”
“Bloody idiot ... You raped me. I will file
a complaint with the police. ”
“Well ... You are saying I raped you?”
“You .... Who else..? "
Salome was furious.

Swami stood up.
He took off his clothes.
“Look, you look.”
Salome was shocked.
Swami did not have a penis.
"Can I attack you with a device I do not
have?"
Salome felt dizzy.

Swami is a woman. The woman with masculine features.

Salome's finger unknowingly touched the ejaculate.

How did this happen?

"There is so much in the universe that ordinary people do not know. What do you all know? You spend time digging up a mobile phone invented by someone and shouting that it is the universe. "

Swami said sarcastically while wearing mund.

He went inside and came with a small bottle.

Inside was a long, thin copper plate rolled up.

"This will fulfill your need."

Salome was stunned.

She bought that bottle automatically.

"Your clothes are in that corner. Take it and go quickly. "

"Iso, shall I go alone?"

"Yes."

"Oh, how can I go alone?" "

"Then he will come down."

"Who?"

"Didn't anyone bring you here?"

"Chintan?"

"Chindano kundano...he is at the bottom of the hill."
Uttaswamy said.
Salome quickly changed clothes.
She checked the bag.
Nothing was stolen.
There was Rs 1.5 lakh in it.
Considered a fee for witchcraft.
That's all there is to it.
Salome came in front of Swami.
Swami looked at her abdomen.

Chapter 7

Salome felt as if Uttaswamy's keen eyes were penetrating inside.
Also, it feels like something is moving inside the abdomen.
As if coming to vomit
Salome vomited.
A yellow liquid came out of his mouth.
Swami asked her:
"Do you go to church?"
"Yes."
"It's okay to go to church. But do not eat the holy bread."
"What is that?"
"I do not know what to say,"
He said.
Salome was confused.

She wiped her lips with a towel.
Then she opened the bag and took a bundle of currency and handed it to Swami.
"My dignity is gone. But here it is. "
"What an honor you have gone through .... Tell me you're really lucky. "
"What is that?"

"You are the mother of great power."
Utta Swami mysteriously laughed.
Salome did not understand that.
"Here's the money."
"I don't want money. I do not need these pieces of paper. It's for you. Take it away. "
Salome put the currency back in the bag.

"What should that bottle do?"
"Keep it in a safe place in your house where no one can see it. In forty-one days, what you intended will happen. If not, come again. "
Uthaswamy said that and grinned.

Salome said in her mind that although what she had intended had not happened; she would never come here again. Salome began to descend the mountain.
Chintan was waiting at the bottom of the hill.
Salome looked up.
Swami is looking at her.
Chintan had started walking when he saw Salome.
Salome hurried to follow him.

She wanted to ask Chintan the secrets of Uttaswamy. Uthaswamy, who grew a beard, mustache, and hair, was obsessed with how she became a woman. Or was the event his magic? In any case, there was no program to ask Chintan about Uttaswamy's secrets. Because Chintan was going very fast. That is, Salome also wondered if Chintan was walking away without catching her questions.

It was no late to reach the intersection.
She gave the money to Chintan
A jeep was getting ready to leave.
Salome quickly got into the jeep.
The jeep started moving along the hillside.

ooooooo

"I'm coming from the shooting set of Lalettan's movie."
Everyone on the bus could hear Neelima Panicker talking on the phone.
They listened in vain.
"Location ... its Hosur. I am coming to Ernakulam by bus. "
Neelima caressed her copper-colored bobbed hair with her finger.

It was slapping the old man nearby in the face.

He was thrilled to smell its shampoo.

When she called, he was watching Neelima Panicker's lipsticked lips tremble.

Neelima continued talking.

"When you come to Ernakulam, can you pick me up from the stand? I thought I would take a bus to Pala tomorrow morning after staying tonight at your flat in Kundannur. "

Sandeep was on the other side.

"Okay...you come here with courage. Anyway, there is no more time in this flat. "

"Oh, it's going to fall apart. When should it be changed? "

"I have to get out of here in two weeks. I got the notice today. "

"What a tragedy, isn't it ...?"

"To whom to tell. Come on anyway. "

Sandeep hung up the phone.

It was morning.

He woke up hearing his mobile phone call of the Neelima.

She's coming straight here.

Salome was the one to fill the gap left.

As he looked around, Salome's shawl and pink bra were scattered on the floor. "Didn't she take any of this ... did she forget to put it on ..?"
Sandeep picked it up and hid it on the shelf.

Then he went into the bathroom and stood under the shower.
The water began to beat gently on his head.
He imagined the lips of the Neelima Panikker below his waist and stood motionless.
Half an hour later he drove to the White Hub.

Chapter 8

Neelima got off a Bangalore Volvo bus.
"I need to eat something bro...I've hungry and my gut is burning."
Neelima said as she got into the car.
Sandeep drove the car straight to the restaurant.
The restaurant was less crowded.
"A Kuzhimanti and an alpha ..."
Neelima ordered.
"You have to pay the money."
"Anyway, will you pay anything, idiot? Tell me what you want." "
"I wish I could have fried an elephant ...... terrible hunger ....."
"Hello, waiter...gives this scholar a loaf of bread and spaghetti ... and gives him the whole bill ..."
Nileema called.
"Do not insult me. This is a shop I am familiar with."
Kuzhimanthi and Alpha came.
Sandeep also ordered the same.
Sandeep was watching with curiosity as he saw Neelima attacking Kuzhimanthi.

"Hello, Didn't Lalettan give you anything to eat there?"
"Then Superstar Tapioca. "
Nileema chuckled.
"Just Tapioca ... sorry ... what about the heroine ... who was the heroine?"
"Or that feminist level Mandakini."
"Which item is the one that ties the hair in the knot and puts the glasses on it?"
"That's it."
"God. Will the film succeed if all these are made heroines...? "
"Performance under coverage."
Neelima said this and snatched the chicken leg from the Kuzhimanthi and bit it.
"So popular?"
"No one is looking. If the film runs or not... the cash goes to some stupid expatriate... called brand equity. "
"Are you tired of seeing this costume?"
"Tired ..? I enjoy watching. Three or four scenes in this movie. We will leave it after that. Then soap the production controller and jump to the next picture. No commitment. "
"What are you doing to soap the production controller?"
"Everyone does."

"What?"
"Idiot...don't you know?"
"No, I do not know."
"Undressed Welcome."
"By the way ..?"
"I'm anxious to tell you, you're great actor honey. You can act in the movie too. "
"Are there any suitable production controller ladies for that ...?"
"No   ... there are giant guys   ... not enough?"
Neelima Panicker said it and laughed out loud.

After the meal, they went straight to their flat in Kundannur.
Sandeep said in the car driving.
"I am going to direct a film."
"Name?"
"She is a Madalasa ...!"
"Which picture?"
"An A certificate ..."
"Isn't all that time over ...!"
"Tell me about tonight ... Heroine Neelima Panicker ..."
Sandeep pinched her thigh.
She burst out laughing.

Chapter 9

Salomi got off the train at Tripunithura.
Got a Thodupuzha fast passenger from Chatharippalam.
It was a good rush.
Hardly got a place to stand.
Something is rolling in my abdomen.
No, it's lying in the abdomen.
The swelling of the abdomen is clearly known in a day.
Salome felt frightened when she remembered.
What a spear this.
While she was thinking, the bus was approaching Kolancherry after Thiruvankulam.
It was half past five in the evening when she got off the bus at Kollencherry.
The intersection was well crowded.
The house is on the route to Mazhuvannur from there.
Salome calls an auto.
"Kandathil Bungalow ..."
She said.
Everyone knows the Bungalow.

A large bungalow in the middle of a five-acre backyard.

Homestead with Cardamom, cocoa and coconut.

There are other workers for agriculture. There is also a person for housework. Sebastian still controls all the work and looks after the math and things. He does so in a wheelchair. Salome is not allowed to interfere in the calculations. But Salome takes the money with some fraud and deception. Eight years after their marriage. Salome's father was a laborer. Her mother had already fallen ill and died. Salome is only one daughter of them. Poverty was the only thing his father, who occasionally went to work, brought with him. She was married to Sebastian when she was in her twenties. He is forty years old. That is, the groom is twenty years older than the bride. Sebastian's father Mammon had two children. Sebastian and Williams. Williams is younger. A bad guy. His father kicked him out of the house. There are so many cases in his name. Williams left for California. Within eight years, Father Mammon and Mother Mary went to the cemetery. Sebastian and Salome had no children. Because Salome knows better. She met a friend via Facebook when her body's recurring needs increased. His name is Sandeep. He is everything to Salome. Salome shows all this adventure in order to bring him to life.

Auto came and stopped in front of the bungalow.
Salome handed the car to the driver, took the bag and the box, and left.
The gate was open.
She did not see any workers there.
Chacko and Janamma go only in the evenings.
They all left early.
Salome hurried up the stairs and into the house.
It is an old style bungalow.
Two storey house.
The house is open.
There is no movement anywhere.
Neelima went to the bedroom.
Sebastian is in a wheelchair facing the window.
"Hey... You are bored ...?"
Salome greeted.
Sebastian did not speak.

Salome took off her top and bra and threw her on the bed.
Wearing only jeans, she looked in the closet mirror.
Nipples black.
She was shocked.
The abdomen is badly pushed.
She put her hand on it.
Something is brewing inside.
She had a tremor.
That's when she remembered about that copper plate.
She opened the bag and took it out.
She looked to see if Sebastian was there and put the copper plate of the bottle in a place not easily visible on the shelf.
Sebastian still doesn't mind.
Didn't he know I came?
"Hello, is it a quarrel sir ...?"
Salome hugged him from behind.
Her hugged hands suddenly got wet.
She looked down.
Blood.
The blood flows like a river.

There is a knife stuck in the chest exactly in the heart.
The heart is splitting and the blood is rushing.
Salome jumped back in shock.
Sebastian has been murdered.
Utta Swamy so terrible?
It happened when she returned from Swami.
But how will she contain this?
Salome felt like she was going crazy.
She sighed and heard a voice behind her.
She looked shocked.
A man with copper color hair.
He grinned, showing his dirty teeth.
He is about thirty-five years old.
Williams!
Salome's lips quivered.

Chapter 10

"A little surprise ..!"
Williams laughed silently.
He looked at Salome's exposed breasts.
She saw it and covered her chest with both hands.
Williams slammed the door and unbuttoned his shirt.
"I'm not preaching the gospel in California, I'm working there smuggling hashish, marijuana, and brown sugar. And the work of adding women to the English men for sex. I will also work as a gunman and shooter. "
He laughed as ugly as the villains in Hollywood movies.
"When my brother dies, all the property goes to his wife ...The property was made by my father and mother ..? I will not allow a woman beggar from anywhere to enjoy this property. Better yet, am I going to marry my brother's wife? "
"How dare you do all this evil?"

Salome mustered up the courage to resist.

"Oh...oh...a holy saint... cools dear ...!"

Williams pulled off his shirt and threw it away.

The red body with the tattoo was strong.

Salome walked back in fear.

She knocked on the bed and fell backward.

Williams instantly unbuttoned her jeans and pulled them down.

Salome was completely naked.

He spread both arms of Salome and leaned over her.

The smell of cigarettes wafted from his mouth.

She felt as if something was working on Salome's body.

Something like what happened in Uthaswamy's prayer room last night.

Lust began to creep into her.

The effect of Mandarayakshi.

Her breasts were full and swollen.

The abdomen was heavy.

The buttocks became enlarged.

The thighs were as thick as the thighs of a banana.

The hair was thick and full of weight.
Williams was unaware of these changes.
He was busy taking off his jeans.
Salome suddenly grabbed him and pulled him closer.
Williams was shocked.
She had the power of ten men.

She tore Williams' jeans with her fingers.
"Lord, you ...!"
Williams began to speak in astonishment, but he could not finish.
Before that, his lips were on Salome's lips.
Her wrists twitched as she hugged his ribs.
His waist tightened with heavy thighs.
Williams' feet slipped as he stepped on Sebastian's blood, which was floating on the floor.
Williams has had many women. But he has never had such an experience with a woman. All the women he had gotten cried in front of his lust and just backed away.
This left Williams completely distraught.
"Salome ...!"
He tried to say.

But he was wandering at the peak of indescribable orgasm, not knowing what to do. In the meantime, he had an ejaculation. With that, his interest was shattered. Then he tried to jump out of Salome's hands anyway. That angered Salome's Yakshi. If a Yakshi does not receive lust from a human being, she will not retreat without breaking his heart and drinking his blood.

Salome, aroused, pushed him down from above her.

Williams slammed into the floor with a thud.

She jumped out of bed.

Williams tried to get up.

He could barely swim in Sebastian's blood on the floor.

Salome came and stood in front of him as Rudra.

He saw that lustful look.

It was not the same Salome he had seen before.

The form of intense lust of a woman with thick thighs, wide waist, large breasts, and buttocks forgetting hair.

She spread both her legs and sat on his waist.

Then he dipped his fingers under the ribs.
Sharp nails dipped into the green flesh.
Williams burst into tears.
She snatched up his beating heart with a laugh.

Then she greedily bit it
Blood gushed.
Her body was drenched in blood.
She stuck out her tongue and drank the blood.
There was blood all over the room.
The smell of fresh flesh and hot blood filled the air.

Chapter 11

Dark is in the room when Salome opened her eyes.
Adhesion of blood around her.
She does not remember how many hours she lay unconscious.
She got up and sees the room.
What I saw then was shocking.
Williams' naked body as his chest split open and his heart pounded out.
Sebastian's body is in a wheelchair next.
Blood floods throughout the room.
Salome looked at her own body.
The whole naked body is bathed in blood.
She tried to calm down.
Both brothers are killed in this room.
They are the two heirs of the Kandathil clan.
This is what the outside world knows.
Something has to be done.
Salome's intellect began to work.

She looked at the clock.
It's ten o'clock at night.

Williams comes to harass him around 6:30 or 7 p.m.

That is, he lost consciousness for three and a half hours.

In the meantime, something happened to Williams.

He was killed.

No matter what happens next, face it.

She went outside and closed the room securely.

Then she went to another bedroom and took a good bath.

She rubbed her abdomen while standing in the shower.

It's swollen again.

Something very powerful was coming down from above them.

She wrapped a gown around her and slowly made coffee.

She picked up her mobile and dialed a number.

Sandeep's number.

When the mobile rang in Sandeep's pocket, he came to the car park of his flat with Neelima Panikkar in the car.

Seeing that it was Salome's call, he answered the phone.

"Dear, I want to see you right away."
Sandeep realized that there was something seriously wrong with Salome's voice as it was very serious.
Neelima is sitting next to him with lust.
If this phone call was made by someone else, he would have been fired.
But he could not quarrel with Salome. Salome is the key to her multi-million dollar fortune. She is supposed to be his wife tomorrow.
He can't talk much because Neelima is sitting nearby.
"I will come right away."
He quickly hung up the phone.
"Néelima, do something. Hold the key now... I'll come when you open the apartment and come in fresh. I urgently need to see a party. "
When Neelima heard this, she became angry.
"What the hell are you doing, Sandeep?"
"Listen to what I have to say. It's essential. Life problem."
"Oh, one of his life problems."
Neelima angrily took the keys and walked out towards the elevator without even looking back.

Sandeep immediately turned the car.
The road was not very busy as it was past ten at night.
It took about half an hour to reach Kolancherry via Thiruvankulam via Tripunithura.
The gate of the bungalow was lying open at the scene.
Salome opened the door before Sandeep got out of the car and rang the calling bell.

Sandeep thought Salome in a white gown was gorgeous.
He hugged her tightly.
"You just took a bath now."
He whispered in her ear.
Salome felt like something was rippling inside her.
She abruptly pushed him away and controlled herself.
"What happened?"
Sandeep asked angrily.
"Things are serious."
Salome said as she closed the door and hugged him.
"Say something."
"Sebastian is dead."
"Hey...how?"

"Killed."
"Did you kill him?"
Sandeep asked in shock.
"I'm not ... He has a brother ... Williams."
"In California."
"Yes ... that bastard."
"God...didn't you tell the police...then where is he ..?"
"He too died."
"How."
"God knows."
Salome said it lightly and led Sandeep to the bedroom where the murders took place.
She opened the door of that room.

When the light in the room came on, Sandeep's blood was frozen.
The room where the blood flowed.
Williams' body with a broken heart.
Sebastian is dead in a wheelchair.
"Are you scared?"
Salome asked silently.
She turned off the light in the room and slammed the door.
"What do you want to drink?"
Sandeep was bathed in sweat.
"Some hot drink... "

He came quickly and sat down wearily in
the chair in the living room.

Chapter 12

Salome brought whiskey and cold water from the fridge.

She poured it into two cups and handed one to Sandeep.

Sandeep emptied the glass in one sip.

Salome sat quietly in her chair and slowly sipped her liqueur.

Sandeep looked at her.

"Did you do this?"

"Didn't I tell you?"

"Or...this...Williams ..."

Sandeep's voice trailed off.

Salome heard it and stared at him.

"Are you crazy, Sandeep?" Can I do that?"

"Then?"

"I do not know."

"God, his chest is split ... his heart is pulled out and bitten and spit out." "

Sandeep covered his face with his hands.

Salome then said sarcastically:

"If you're scared, get up and leave the place ... a woodpecker that came to help."

Sandeep was insulted by those words.
He nodded silently for a moment and then took the whiskey bottle and poured it into his mouth.
Salome angrily grabbed the bottle.
"What are you going to do? If you drank all this and fainted here, I would have to bury those two bodies and you. Workers will come here tomorrow morning. Something has to be done before that. "
"Tell me what to do?"
"Both bodies should be buried. Come on. "

Salome brought the toolbox from the store room.
"What are you going to do?"
Sandeep asked anxiously
"Come on idiot."
Salome walked into the kitchen.
She grabbed a torch and held it out to Sandeep.
"Hold this."
The two opened the kitchen door and walked out.
Salome came to the front of the biogas plant.

"The lid of this biogas plant should be open. But even if the lid is opened, the body cannot be put in this"
Salome said.

It is a biogas plant with a diameter of two and a half meters.
It is buried in the ground. It is two feet above the ground.
"The nut and bolt are much tightened."
Sandeep inspected the gas plant.
"That's why idiot took this tool kit. Open the lid quickly. ”
Salome lowered her voice and suggested.

She looked around.
Great backyard.
There is no accommodation nearby.
As it is outside the kitchen, no one can see from the road.
Sandeep started unpacking the plant.
It worked out with half an hour of effort.
Salome and Sandeep also put aside its heavy lid.
The stench emanated from within.
Both covered their noses.
“Salome, you are very intelligent.”
Sandeep congratulated.
“Come quickly without time waste.”

Salome quickly dragged Sandeep inside.
She picked up a plastic sheet.
In it, Williams' body was taken.
They both hung it up and put it in the gas plant.
Sebastian's body was buried as well.
Then the lid of the plant was tightly closed.
The blood in the room was completely washed away.

After all, Sandeep said:
"There is blood on our dress. All this must be burned. "
"I can do that."
Salome hurriedly looked at the clock
"It's four o'clock in the morning. You take a shower, put on Sebastian's pants and shirt, and leave quickly. "
"Tell me, what's the plan?"
Sandeep looked into her eyes.

Salome thought for a moment.
"Employees will come. Then I will say that my husband went to Bangalore in the morning. I will say the same even if his clients and friends ask. There will be no unnecessary questions as there are no relatives other than Williams. I'm

leaving in two days. I am telling them, I'm going to Bangalore with my husband. In the meanwhile, if he has to give cash to anyone, it should be settled. Harass those who get cash. The givers do not bother. The worker may entrust Pappachan with the task of looking after the house. Then within a year it should sell nicely and move away. That's my idea. "
"You are intelligent honey."
Sandeep hugged her and kissed her.
Salome felt the pleasure of his kiss spread through her veins badly.
As if something was rushing under the abdomen.
Salome sniffed the danger and withdrew from the embrace.
"Take a quick shower and leave."
Salome told him.
Sandeep went to take a bath.
By the time he got out of the bath, Salome was already making tea.
He drank it and got in the car and left the place.
Salome thought with a sigh.

Chapter 13

Half-past four in the morning.
Salome awoke startled from thinking.
She took off all her clothes and went to the bathroom.
The abdomen is now severely swollen.
This is the semen of the Kandakattan.
Three to four months of growth per day of pregnancy.
Salome was terrified.
By the time he is ten months old, his stomach will have ruptured.
This should be done through abortion.
Not even Sandeep was told.

She opened the shower and stood under the water.
The blood that had clung to her body was washed away.
Salome took a bath, wiped her body, got dressed, and went to sleep.
She quickly slipped into a dream.

Something ancient.

A place is full of black stone pillars with oil wicks burning.
The cry of the Kollikkuravan the bird of death, in the mystery of midnight.
The atmosphere is so intense, perhaps because of the Ashtami on the black moon.
She jumps angrily on the floor where the blood has dried.
A large hearth for Homam in front.
In front of it was a yard with burning stick wicks.
At the back is a tall statue.
The statue of Kandakakattan.
A fierce thing with burning eyes and a long tongue.
A black man is blindfolded near the altar.
He was in the form of Uttaswamy.
That Utta Swamy, the sacrificial animal in a garland speaks nothing. Not even crying.
Dressed in red silk, she was dancing.
The sword flashed in her hand.
Her buttocks and breasts were moving erratically to the rhythm.
Suddenly it felt like something was hooking inside her abdomen.

The dynamism of her dance was disturbed.

The ovum in the uterus ruptures and menstruates with blood coming out of the vagina.
Menstrual blood flowed down her thighs.
It fell on the loom and flowed abnormally into the crematorium.
She was shocked.
The fast has been broken.
Pooja and sacrifice have stopped.
She knelt on the floor.
At that moment a growl was heard.
The sacrificial animal growls.
The strong man in the form of Uttaswamy untied the knot in his hands and laughed heartily.
Then he ran and picked up the sword she had thrown away.
The sword rose and fell at her, bowing in agony, humiliation, and despair.
Her head rolled and fell into the hearth.
Blood gushed from the body.
He collected the blood in a skull that was there and anointed the statue and bowed.

The calling bell was ringing in the front door when Salome woke up from her dream.

She ran and opened the door.

That is Pappachan, the servant.

"Was that you?"

"Oh, a lot of calls. When did madam come? "

"I came at midnight. Husband left for Bangalore at dawn. "

"Oh, sir, what did he do?"

Pappachan turned around in shock.

An ulka flashed inside Salome.

Yet she did not show the fear.

"What's the matter, Papachan?"

"He told me to go to Thodupuzha today. Buy pepper seedlings. We have to give them an advance. "

Salome let out a deep sigh

"Oh, that was it. Husband had said. Tell them to pack the plants. Don't you have their mobile number of them? "

"Yes."

"Call them. The cash may be credited to their account. "

"All right. Please give me the key to that shed. "

Pappachan shook his head.

Salome brought the keys to the workers' shed.
Pappachan walked towards the yard.
Salome sighed in relief.

Chapter 14

Eleven o'clock in the morning.
When Salome arrived at the Sheena Clinic it was pretty busy.
Dr. Sheena is a renowned gynecologist in Thiruvankulam. The Sheena Clinic operates in a two-story building that stands out from the crowd on the street. She is Salome's friend.
Salome waited to get avoid the rush.
Until then she had been looking at WhatsApp.
There are messages from Sandeep.
'Good morning ...drink tea ... ' and other trolls. Salome has no more friends. But good morning content was forwarded to everyone. Then came the reply flow. 'Good morning at eleven o'clock, is it morning now for you? '

By then, the cabin was open and Dr. Sheena came.
"Did you come here? How are you? Is your husband feeling well? "
Salome hurriedly grabbed Sheena's hand and walked into the cabin.

"I have a suspicion!"
"Okay. I can check ... please bed..? "
Salome lay on the bed in the consulting room.
Dr. Sheena examined her.

Salome watched as Sheena's face changed.
"Three months ... What have you not told me yet?"
Sheena asked.
Salome nodded.
She said:
"I have been skeptical for two days."
"If you say you have not known pregnancy for three months, you should be beaten."
Sheena angrily continued:
"If something happened to this baby without your knowledge, you need to take care of it. I'll prescribe some medicine. You get up. "
Dr. Sheena sat down on the chair and started prescribing medicines.
Salome stood up and took her hand.
"Will you quarrel if I say something?"
"What happened?"
"This ...!"

"Is it?"
"I do not want this child."
"Are you crazy Salome, how long have you been waiting to have a baby?"
Dr. Sheena was furious.
Salome wondered what to say.

Would Dr. Sheena believe that this is Kantakatan's baby? Would anyone believe me if I told them that I was pregnant yesterday? Sheena has already said that it will be three months.
"Why are you silent?"
Dr. Sheena asked.
Finally, Salome said:
"It's not Sebastian's."
Dr. Sheena was shocked.
"Then?"
"You don't have to know that,"
Salome said.
Dr. Sheena engaged in consultation.

Salome sat anxiously in the chair with her eyes on Sheena's face.
After a while, Sheena said:
"This is your baby now. Let paternity belong to anyone. You have a husband to tell you anything. My opinion is that this should not be discarded. Not even

Sebastian needs to know about its paternity. ” Sebastian is not going to know about this anymore. Salome's insides were throbbing. She said to Sheena:
“It's not as simple as you think.”
“Then?”
"I cannot say that."
"I know. This is what everyone says about an unintended pregnancy. I have seen so much. You can go. I did not agree to abort it. ”
Dr. Sheena said firmly.

Then, observing them, there was an unusually large black thing sitting above her head on the false ceiling.
Salome's mind sank. She jumped up.
"If you cannot do it ... you are not the only one in this country.”
Salome went out like a storm.
Dr. Sheena was shocked.

Chapter 15

When Salome arrived home, two men were waiting.

Pappachan came running.

"Salome madam, people of the pepper plant group are waiting. The goods have been delivered. "

"Okay, how much is their bill?"

Salome asked.

People from the pepper nursery came closer.

They said:

"One and a half lakh rupees. Six thousand five hundred rupees discount. The rest after eating it.... "

Salome said intermittently.

"If possible, we can settle today. Husband has gone to Bangalore. Email your bank details ... Okay. "

"Okay, madam."

They got in the car.

Salome walked into the house.

She opened her laptop and went into the net bank and checked Sebastian's bank account.

The total is Rs 2.5 lakh.

She thought, if I pay the pepper growers for this, I will get the problem.

It was said in the panic of the time. It was enough to cancel that order. Salome was engrossed in the discussion.

She decided something and stood up.

When she came to the porch, she saw Pappachan and two workers standing in the yard.

"Pappacha"

Salome called.

Pappachan came running.

"What the hell?"

"Where's that pepper seedlings?"

"Or ... didn't it lease the land to Mazhuvannur Kuncheri...there."

"Is that there?"

"There is pepper cultivation."

"Pepper is grown on leased land? God, is my husband crazy? Any crop of paddy, paddy, or banana can be cultivated on the leased land. Wouldn't we be worried if the landlord asked us to vacate the land if we were cultivating pepper? "

"Is this how it is now ...?"

"Um...okay...okay."

Salome shook her head and went inside.

She thinks about what she needed to do to keep the money from going away.

Mary, the housekeeper, came and made rice and curries.
Mary is a woman who asks many questions.
Salome seriously avoided everything.
Every now and then she would go near that biogas plant and look,
Whether there are any signs. Nothing in doubt. Blood stained the night before she secretly burned Sandeep's and her clothes.

She remembered Sandeep as she lay in bed for a nap in the afternoon.
She immediately called him.
Sandeep was saddened by Neelima Panicker's quarrel.
When Sandeep went to his flat in Kundannur in the morning, she had locked the flat and left the place.
She left with the key. At four-thirty in the morning, Sandeep was trapped. He called Neelima's phone. After much effort, she picked up the phone. She was with a friend in Kadavanthara. He had to listen to every bad thing she said.

Finally, he went to her and got the keys to the flat. He slapped Neelima's cheek before leaving. For Neelima, it was unexpected. You cannot tell this story to Salome.

Sandeep was in the office when Salome called.
"What's the matter?"
"Will you come, Sandeep?"
"Hey, is there a problem?"
"I need a little help."
"Small help like yesterday."
Sandeep laughed.
"Pota ..."
Salome was devastated
"Come anyway."
"Come on, honey."
Sandeep put a kiss on the phone.
Then, in the half-cabin on the other side, colleague Selena asked him:
"Why are you playing kiss on the little phone?"
Sandeep bowed his head in shame.

Chapter 16

When he left the office that evening, Sandeep drove straight to Koloncherry, not to Kundannur, but Salome's house.
It was about eight o'clock in the morning when he arrived at Salome's house.
"Let me take a shower and freshen up."
When he arrived, he went to the bathroom.
By the time he got home from the bath, Salome had been making tea.
Sandeep looked at her sarcastically,
"Tea at this time?"
"Then do you drink alcohol at this time instead of tea?"
"I'm glad to hear you say a movie about Christians hugging whiskey at the dinner table."
"Alas, you nairs, you have not seen any alcohol. We Christians are not bathed in alcohol... "
Salome said the same and brought a bottle of whiskey.
Sandeep opened the lid of the whiskey bottle and sniffed
"Nairs do not like whiskey."

"What ...?"
"Oh, haven't you heard vat, made from home?"
"I drank it."
"Hey. When?"
Sandeep was surprised.
Salomi remembered that what was found in Uttaswamy's prayer room was vat.
"Oh, some time?"
Salome nodded.
"Is there any way to get it?"
"For the time being, you drink it."
"Touchings."
"Is fried fish enough?"
"Let's fight."
Salome went to the kitchen and fetched the fried fish.

Sandeep opened the bottle and poured the whiskey into two glasses and added cold water.
A glass gives out towards Salome.
She bought it and zipped it.
"You have to do something for me."
"Tell me what ...?"
"Sebastian had ordered some pepper seedlings."
"And then?"

"The bloody pepper nursery team has supplied the goods today. I have to give them around Rs one and a half lakh. The total amount in Sebastian's account is two and a half lakhs. My case will be a problem if this money goes away. I need money to live anymore. "

"Is that why you are so worried? Tell them you will pay...will pay. Then do not give up the money.

"The pepper seeding order is made by my husband. If it were not for this one situation it would have done so. If they do not get the money, they will put pressure on me to get a husband. That should be a problem. "

"What is the plan for this?"

"There is a plan. Do you know how to ride a scooter? "

"Sure, I can drive any vehicle."

Sandeep looked at Salome and said with a sexual meaning.

"You don't have to drive like that anymore," she said. "

"Okay, just drive your car."

Sandeep said and laughed.

"Then after dinner, we have to go somewhere."

"Let it be ... only not to fight."

"I cannot say for sure. All you have to do is sip whiskey. "
Salome grabbed the bottle and brought it to the minibar.
She lined up dinner at the dinner table.
There was rice, fish curry, banana, and chicken.
Sandeep was drunk and excited.

He washed his hands and hugged Salome from behind, who was serving food.
He rubbed her belly, kissing her shampooed hair.
He felt as if something inside her was shaking violently.
He pulled his hands away in shock.
He forcibly held her back.
"What?"
Salome asked.
Sandeep looked up and down at her.
She was wearing a dark blue velvet nightgown.
"Why is your stomach like this?"
"How?"
"What makes your belly suspiciously swollen?"
Salome has badly in mind but she didn't show it off. She said

"The alcohol is attacked you. You can fight the meals. "
She tried to keep her stomach small. She realized it was bigger than the morning. It is no longer possible to hide it inside clothing.
She sat down in her chair and began to eat.
Sandeep also started eating.
Salome glanced at him.
He noticed she was looking.

Chapter 17

It was ten o'clock at night after dinner.
The road quickly became deserted as it was a hamlet.
Salome changed her dress.
She was wearing a palazzo and a loose top and a monkey cap. In that role, she would not have felt much belly. Sandeep looked at her stomach and sighed.
Salome noticed it.
She quietly brought a kit from the room,
She ordered.
"You start the scooter."
Sandeep started the Activa scooter. It was a three-wheeler used by Sebastian.
Salome was sitting in the back.
"Go to Mazhuvannur. I will tell you the way. It is only half a kilometer from here. "
"Okay, dear."

They found out the location of Kuncheria, which Sebastian had leased.
There were the peppers nursery plants lined up in front of a small shed prepared as a farmhouse.

Salome picked up a bottle with a spray cap from the kit.
She sprayed it on the peppercorns.
"What is this?"
Sandeep asked quietly
"Thinner."
"What is thinner?"
"Well, this is a thinner used for painting. When it falls, the leaves look like they have been infected with scabs. This is the only way to retrieve the item. Then we don't have to pay. "
"Your Wisdom Is Great"
Sandeep congratulated.

They quickly got things done and went back home.
Salome stopped the scooter on the porch and got off.
"But Sandeep, do you go ..."
Sandeep got off the scooter and jumped.
"Do not tell the same story. Don't I have to go to Kundannur again tonight? That's what happened. "
Sandeep ran and entered the house.

Salome followed furiously.
She was scared.

Tonight will be scary if Sandeep himself is touched.

When lust is born in her, mandarayakshi wakes up.

If the man in front of her is not satisfied, he will have a terrible end. That's what happened to Williams. It has been proven that it is true that a man cannot subdue the Mandara Yakshi through sex.

But if Sandeep stays here tonight, he will be in my bed. But it will end in disaster.

Suddenly a light flashed in her head. An amphetamine can save Sandeep. He may be carrying such a sexual stimulant.

She was relieved to hear that.

When Salome looked, Sandeep closed all the doors himself.

He looks like a greedy beast.

Salome went to the bedroom and opened the closet to change clothes.

Sandeep came to the bed with the door closed.

Salome looked at him.

He laughed mischievously.

She asked seriously.

"What ... what is your purpose?"

"The prince has come before that castle, breaking down all barriers."

"How many times have I jumped the fort wall ...?"

"Isn't that ... the thrill of remembering the princess I own?" "

When Sandeep said that, Salome took off her palazzo and top and searched for a nightgown in the wardrobe with nominal underwear.

This time Sandeep got up and hugged her tightly.

Salome felt as if something were shaking all over her.

A rash spreads from the big toe to the scalp.

She regained consciousness and pushed him away.

Sandeep was taken aback.

She asked angrily:

"Are you leaving to die ...?"

"What?"

Sandeep asked leaving the end.

Salome was confused, not knowing what to say next.

Sandeep will run away from here if things are told in detail. Then I will never get him again in my life. And he has enough to say and spread. She took the idea that had already flashed in her head and let it out.

"Do you have any amphetamines in your hand?"

Sandeep burst out laughing.

"What is your problem? Is this why you rejected me. Hello silly girl, you need amphetamine if you want to have sex with me. What are you, Are you a pornstar? "

"Hello rascal ... not me, you need amphetamine ..."

"Are you crazy, Salome?"

"It simply came to our notice then. I'm crazy...or lust crazy. I will forget myself if I catch that madness. If you do not satisfy me, I will break your heart and drink your blood. "

Salome uttered those words as if she were drunk.

Sandeep, however, took it as a joke. He pulled down his jeans.

The source of power that was pulsing in his waist was awake.

When she saw it, she lost all control.

She also took off her nominal underwear.

Sandeep saw her swollen abdomen.
He touches it with suspicion.
Something moved inside.
A face appeared on the skin.
Sandeep jumped back.
A magical aroma permeated the air.
Salome reached out and touched him.

Chapter 18

A definite feeling seeping through his body.

He looked at Salome with half-closed eyes.

It was not Salome.

A beautiful young woman.

He had never seen such a beauty.

Heavy breasts

Large black nipples

Banana trunk-sized thighs.

Broad buttocks and narrow waist.

Hair that forgets the buttocks.

Lustful eyes and bloody lips.

She excitedly grabbed his face and pulled him closer to her.

When she touched his lips to him, he realized that all the energy in his body was concentrated in that source of energy in his waist.

The next moment the energy radiated out like a hot flame.

Sandeep was pushed to the unconscious.

Her face changed when she found out he had ejaculated.

White long teeth appeared on the corners of her angry mouth.
The fingernails grew and sharpened.
She grabbed him and hit him on the floor.
Then she jumped on him with a terrible laugh.
With a craving for blood, the sharp claws of her fingers pierced the flesh beneath his ribs.
She tore the meat layer effortlessly and pulled out that beating heart.
The arteries and veins pulled her out of the intertwined strands.
Then she held up that blood-soaked human heart above her mouth.
She drank a lot of blood like a maniac.

ooooooooo

Uthaswamy was meditating in a small hut on the top of Mutharamala.
Anoop, the dog, was lying on the edge of the room looking at him.
He could see the Karnapisasini whispering something in Uttaswamy's right ear.
Uttaswamy's lips were still chanting the mantra of Karnapisasini.

The Karnapisasini said:

"As long as there is semen in her abdomen, Mandarayakshi will not leave her. The semen of the Kandakattan is born as the Keeldwaja. It is the incarnation of Keelakan, one of the thirty-two Ketu, the sons of Rahu. All the human men who try to sex her will be killed. Human men cannot satisfy Mandarayakshi, the fourteenth goddess in Sex. But something impure is approaching the Keeladwaja. Wait carefully. "

The Karnapisasini has disappeared.

Uttaswamy awoke from his meditation.

His lips murmured

"An unclean thing that approaches the Keeladwaja."

Anoop murmuring.

Uthaswamy looked at him sharply.

"Shut up ... the Karnapisa is not hidden ... it's still present. Do not disturb the Goddess with the sound of a dog. "

Anoop calmed down.

Uthaswamy looked at him curiously.

Then she called him sympathetically.

"Anoop ... come here ..."

He refused to come. He is quarreled.

Uthaswamy got up and shook him.

Suddenly the old man lost control and
hugged him and cried
"My dear ..."
Anoop's ancestral memories roared.
It was not too far away.
Birth of a rebellious son!

Chapter 19

Salome woke up.
She was lying on top of Sandeep's body bathed in blood.
Salome screamed and jumped up.
Then she suddenly regained her composure and suppressed her cry.
She tried to remember what had happened.
The man who loved me has fallen victim to the mandara yakshi that lives in me.
Sandeep was her hope. She thinks.
He did all these things in the belief that he would be with me.
What to do next.
If not Sandeep, I will get another man.
Men will still come to me.
But they cannot sex with me forever.
What a growing pregnancy in me.
What is the purpose of the mandara that excites me?
Will these forces save me?
Or will it erase me forever, as it did mercilessly slay all my loved ones?
They are merciless demonic forces.

I need salvation.
I have to do something about it.

She looked at the clock.
The time is two o'clock at night.
Salome went into the bathroom thinking of something.
The dried blood stains on the body were washed away.
The abdomen is very protruding.
She looked at her reflection in the floor mirror in the bathroom.
The growth of that abnormal fetus is very fast.
The nipples are black.
Except for the black of the nipples and the unusual belly, there was no particular damage to the shape she had maintained.
Only if it is more beautiful.
This beauty came to her mind probably because of the presence of the very beautiful Mandarayakshi in her body.
But when lust awakens, does something change in his body?
Swollen buttocks and heavy thighs may be present.
Breasts get bigger.
Dense long hair will also appear.

Or is it just my feeling?

But the man who arrives in front of her with a passion for sex is brutally murdered for failing to satisfy sex himself.
Then he forgets himself.
He cannot remember what is happening.
But the state of her body and mind, where lust is awakened, presents a great thrill.
Abnormality of indefinable sex.
The climax of the process is impossible for any human being.

Salome wanted to capture that lust in herself once She caressed her breasts in such a way that she lusted after herself.
She looked at the black nipples protruding in the floor mirror and tried to wake up Rati Devi who was sleeping inside.
Her fingers went down, caressing her swollen abdomen.
The lust blossomed in my mind due to the caress, but it was only as if it happened naturally.

The lustful Mandarayakshi did not wake up in her with unspeakable sexual desire.

Salome sat on the bathroom floor in frustration.
She was convinced of the truth.
Mandarayakshi appears only in front of a naked man who is sexually aroused.

Salome, who had been thinking for a long time, suddenly thought of Sandeep's body and got up in shock, and finished the bath.
She wiped her head, wears a nightgown, and went to the bedroom.
She took courage.
She decided to face this situation alone.
She was devastated to learn that the man who had been helping her so far was dead.
But this is not the time to grieve.

She wrapped Sandeep's body in a plastic sheet.
Then she dragged it back through the kitchen.
The light was turned off. But there was a good moon.

He took the spanner from the toolbox and opened the lid of the biogas plant.
It had a good weight.
She opened the lid and tilted it.
Then a strong stench came out.
She felt like vomiting.
She covered her mouth.
Both bodies are beginning to rot.
They will disappear in a week. Due to the intense chemical reaction in that plant, the bio-waste will quickly decompose into gas. Within months, even the bones will melt away.
The plant was taller than Salome's shoulder.

She picked up Sandeep's body which was lying on the ground in a plastic sheet and put it inside the plant.
Then she tightened the lid.
The plastic sheet and cemented kitchen yard were washed and cleaned with a hose.
After washing the room, Salome breathed a sigh of relief.
It was two o'clock in the morning.
Somewhere she could hear the terrifying screams of a Kollikkuravan the bird of death.

Is death looming over the house like a
beast?
Salome sought refuge in another
bedroom.
She fell asleep while lying down.

Chapter 20

Salome woke up in the morning when Pappachan came and rang the bell.

She tied her hair and looked at the clock.

Eight and a half o'clock.

She thought.

What to say to Pappachan.

She came and opened the door.

Then he asked:

"What's the matter Pappachan?"

"The people of that pepper nursery are calling."

"So early in the morning. Pappacha, they have no sleep. Are they afraid we will not pay? "

"At first they said that they would give the seedlings only if we paid the full amount.

"We have to see if the seedlings are good. Aren't we customers? "

"Give it to me."

"Well, I'll give it to you ... I want to see the pepper seedling."

"Good original pepper seedling."

"I'll see it ... Pappachan call an auto."

"Can't madam take that car?"
"Towards that wild area... can you call an auto suddenly?"
Salome's voice grew louder.
Pappachan murmured something and picked up the mobile.

Within seconds the auto arrived.
Salome came in a white big Kurtha. She got into the auto.
Pappachan followed them with his old Kinetic Honda.

They arrived at the farm.
Pappachan was shocked to see pepper seedlings lined up with white spots around the farm shed.
"Koche, is this a spot disease?"
He put his hand on his chest.
Salome acting with anger:
"Is that why Pappacha told me to pay? Scammers go down with every tactic to catch people. Is money wasted? "
"Let me call them one."
Pappachan started calling angrily.
Salome quickly got back into the auto.
She was happy that the problem was solved.

Maid Katrina made puttu and eggs curry for breakfast.

Salome said as she enjoyed breakfast:

"This egg curry is good, Katrina." "

"It was made in the style of Malabar people. My doubt was whether you would like it. "

"It's super."

"Sir does not like eggs curry. It is made for you madam because your husband is not here. Or I would have made chicken curry. Where did he go, madam? He is not a person who goes away out even for a day. "

Katrina asked.

Salome stumbled but she did not show it.

"Didn't I say He is in Bangalore?"

"But what's up there?"

"Want to tell you about the event there?"

Salome suddenly became angry.

Katrina frowns:

"I don't care. I don't care. I just asked. He tells Pappachan if he's going anywhere. "

"Does he have to tell you all to go somewhere?"

"No baby ... no more arguing over it. I didn't ask anything."

As soon as Katrina said that, Salome cooled down.

"We want to start a homemade chocolate business. Sales are made online. That too via Amazon. Ichayan has gone to Amazon's Bangalore office to talk about it. "

"That's right ... that's good ... then the whole company is starting, isn't it?"

"Um ..."

"My daughter passed BCom first class. She leaves it at home. Madam, please tell to him to give her a job. "

"Um. Let me tell you, I'm going to Bangalore in two days. "

Then who will protect the house? Is the house closed?"

"The house will be closed."

"What about me?"

"Katrina should not have come."

Salome paused and continued.

"We can come here and call Katrina. Then you come. Anyway, I'll tell him about Katrina's daughter. "

Salome stood up and washed her hands. Then she saw a small newspaper lying on the table.

Word of God!

Is a Christian gospel newspaper.

An ad in it caught Salome's attention.

"... Fr. Gregorios Anastasi, who provides miraculous healing.

Prayer cures all diseases including cancer.

Miracles that bind all plagues, demons, and ghosts on the index finger. Those who come in person should call and come. "

"Good. The phone number is also given. "

Salome walked into the bedroom with the newspaper.

Chapter 21

"Your son has been afflicted with evils like Kundala devil and Kulalakappiri. Didn't you say he had no problem until he was two years old? Science calls it autism in Malayalam. There is nothing on earth that the Holy God cannot pay. "

Fr Gregorios Anastasi told the couple in front of him.

Father was a strong man in his forties.

Handsome with black curly hair.

Several award plaques are stacked on his back shelf.

The couple looked at their father with adoration.

A twelve-year-old boy is sitting next to them.

Father continued:

"Society often celebrates many illnesses. Homosexuality is a disease. It's a special kind of mental illness. But what does society do? Instead of treating such people, it has been made law by a court order. Courts issue stupid orders that should not be questioned if a man marries his wife. Similarly, a group of transgender people was once called Hijadas. The section where the man dresses as a woman. Boys who have been sexually abused during adolescence are more likely to wear such costumes. There are men and women of all sex, whether homosexual or not. There are such moods. It is a disease. When such patients rule the country their madness becomes law. It is a tragedy that has always been repeated in history. "

Father Gregorios Anastasi spoke enthusiastically as a speaker.
He got up and put his hand on the boy's head.
"I heard a sound from heaven like the roar of a waterfall, like the roaring of thunder. A lamb stands on top of Mount Zion. And with him one hundred and forty-four thousand. His name and his father's name are written on their foreheads. You will be healed and you will be healed and you will be healed. "
As soon as the father said that, the child fell unconscious.
His parents take him.

"Take him away. I will pray to the Lord
for him. "
The parents came out of the room with
the child.

It was very crowded outside.
A queue has formed.
There is a separate counter for giving
tokens and collecting fees.
From there, anyone has to pay a fee of
100 rupees and buy a token to see
Father.
The bell rang for the next person.
The token number was also announced
through the mic.
The token number man entered through
the crowd at the door.
Suddenly a young woman rushed in,
pushing everyone away
"Father must save me."
It was Salome.
"I am the token number holder."
Said the person with the token.
Salome pushed him away and stood in
front of Father.
Those waiting their turn also shouted.
Father asked her:
"Did you take the token?"
"No. "

"But go and get the token and stand in the queue."
"Father, my case is serious. Is essential.
"

"All are essential. You go and get the token. "
Father said to her and invited the token holder.
"Father, listen to what I have to say."
"You go out. I will give you a chance to tell. "
When Father finished, Salome stepped out in despair.

The crowd at the door greeted her with laughter.
A grandmother asked aloud:
"Why did you get rejected in a big way ...?"
"Go to hell old lady ..."
Salome said and hurried out.
She did not stop to pick up the token.
She angrily picked up the car from the parking area.
The car sped off.

It was about four o'clock in the evening when Father Gregorios Anastasi was ending the consulting. The maid served him food in the dining room. Father's only food from morning to four o'clock was milk with Horlicks, which he drank occasionally. Felix sat at the counter, counting the bundles of currency and stacking them in bundles.

Father washed his hands and came to the dinner table and slowly started eating bread and beef curry.

Then Father's phone rang.

Is an anonymous number.

Father picked up the phone and put it to his ear.

"Tell me ..."

It was Salome.

Father Gregorios Anastasia was shocked to hear what she had to say.

A pregnancy that grows into days us the growth of months..!

Its circumstances..!

Salome summed up the information.

He finished his meal and washed his hands.

"I will come at night. The Lord will save you. The devil will leave you tonight. "

Father Gregorios Anastasi said it and hung up.

He looked at the crucifix on the wall:

"Are you acting so fast? Has the Antichrist arrived...? "
Then an unusual wind blew through the window curtains and into the room.

Chapter 22

At ten o'clock at the night, Father Gregorios arrived at the house of Anastasi Salome.

Arrived in his white sedan car.

No attendants.

Salome welcomed him inside.

She was wearing a nightgown made of blue velvet.

The priest looked down at her.

His eyes fell on the swollen abdomen, which was a hindrance to the beauty of a beautiful young woman.

"What does Father want to drink?"

Salome asked.

"Nothing."

"Sit down Father."

Priest, however, did not sit down. He looked around.

That mind was like a police officer looking for criminals and witches looking for evil spirits.

It seemed to Priest that some spirits were called by his name.

The priest felt as if someone inside was asking him to leave quickly.
But this is what Priest said to Salome.
"Close that main door ... turns off all the lights in the room."
Salome obeyed Priest's words.
"Come and stand in front of me."
He told Salome.
"I have the power to ward off evil spirits ... no matter what the devils."
Priest's confident words made her courageous.

Salome came and stood in front of Priest.
The priest put his hand on her forehead and said:
"Fear God and give him glory."
"Amen."
Salome replied.

He then placed his hand on her protruding abdomen.
Something shook violently inside his stomach.
Salome sighed in pain.
The priest felt that movement well.
"Take off your clothes."
Priest asked.

Salome unbuttoned her velvet nightgown.

There was no underwear inside.

Father Gregorios Anastasi's heart rate increased.

He tried to pray with his hand on her naked belly but forgot the words of the prayer.

Salome was staring into Priest's eyes.

It was as if something powerful was sprouting under her abdomen and spreading all over her body.

The priest's body was sweating.

Lust gripped Priest like a snake.

He untied the holy dress.

Priest realizes that Salome has undergone significant transformations.

Dense hair grows to the buttocks.

The priest was amazed at the shape of her buttocks and the beauty of her body.

She stretched out her right hand and ran her fingers down Priest's chest.

The priest felt as if sparks of electricity were passing through his body.

He unknowingly knelt in front of her naked body.

She took his heavy thigh and placed it on Priest's shoulder.

The priest felt the smell of hot vagina hit him in the face.

"What do you call me?"
She asked softly.
Father Gregorios Anastasio's mouth was dry.
When no words came out, she repeated the question.
The Priest said with a shudder
"SA ... lo ..... Mi."
She laughed.
The laughter was like the ringing of a beautiful bell.
"No ... Do you think I'm Salome?"
".... E ... no... "
"Then ...?"
"I don't know."
She laughed again when she heard Father's panicked voice.
"This strong voice of yours is beautiful. Let me embrace it. "
She ran her fingers through Father's curly hair and lifted him.
Father stood in front of her like an obedient boy.
Her fingers traveled through Father's naked abdomen.

Father Gregorios Anastasio was in a state of panic.

She was touched by the strong state of celibacy.

She hugged Father tightly and started sucking his lips.

Father unknowingly hugged her.

The intense flow of energy of celibacy began to flow from the waist like a fire.

She raised her right leg and twisted it.

Father felt as if something bright was exploding on her forehead as she touched her genitals and it descended through the spinal cord and reached the Kundalini.

At that moment, the ejaculation erupted, raising the trumpet of death.

She stood still for a few moments.

Father fainted in the bliss of heaven.

Her expression changed. Hands relaxed.

Father's head fell to the floor as she removed her twisted leg.

She jumped on the Preist in anger.

Chapter 23

Pappachan arrived at the bungalow around 8.30 am. The gate was locked.

He stumbled in through the gap in the south wall.

Walked around the house.

The house is also locked.

But the car and two-wheeler are on the porch.

Pappachan called maid Katrina on the phone.

"Didn't you come to the bungalow?"

"I came and saw the gate locked." "

"Didn't madam tell you anything?"

"No, but she said they would go to Bangalore. No one saw her go so fast. "

"She never told me anything."

Pappachan got angry.

"What is this?"

"I don't know anything. He's calling me on his mobile usually. It is unknown at this time what he will do after leaving for Bangalore. This is how we starve, Katrina. "

While Pappachan was saying that, another call came on the phone.

"Katrina, someone is calling. Let's see. "
Pappachan cut off Katrina's call and
took a new one.

On the other side was Salome.
"Papachan, its Salome. I left in the
morning. Keep going to Bangalore. We
will come back in two weeks. Take a look
at the farm. "
"But the gate is locked."
"Doesn't Pappachan have a spare key?"
"No. "
"It does not matter. Let me come and
see. "
"All right."
Pappachan murmured and hung up the
call.
Salome smiled and switched off her
mobile and put it in the car seat.
She was driving fast.

National Highway 66 was close to the
city of Kozhikode.
She parked her white I2o car in a busy
area near Pachakil Junction. The car
belonged to Father Gregorios Anastasio.
The road was crowded with school
children, staff, and vehicles and no one
had time to pay attention to anyone.

Salome took her backpack from her car, slung it over her shoulder, and boarded a private bus from a nearby stop.

"Malaparambu Junction."

She told the conductor.

He bought the money and cut the ticket.

"Someone give a seat to this pregnant woman."

The conductor asked the passengers.

Someone vacated the seat.

She sat comfortably in it.

Eleven o'clock in the morning.

Southern Thiruvankulam Police Station.

The station was busier than usual.

SI Jayaraman is in an urgent meeting with ASIs Pradeep and James.

"The Thripunithura CI has come out here. The commissioner also called. The disappearance of Father Gregorios Anastasio must be stopped as soon as possible. Missing since last night. No information. The man disappeared with the car. The phone is switched off."

Meanwhile, a police officer came to Deepak and hurriedly showed his head.

"Sir CI has come."

"Hello Deepak, that Felix is there, isn't he? Father's secretary. "

"Yes sir … District Panchayat President Dominic has also come."

"Okay."

By then, the CI and the district panchayat president had come to the SI's cabin.

"Things got to the point where. Is there any progress? "

When CI Mohandas came, he inquired.

The sub-inspector emptied the chair for the circle Inspector and stood up politely "Father has been missing since last night."

"I know, I know. Did you do any investigation? "

Secretary Felix was questioned. He does not know anything. "

"Call him."

CI suggested.

ASI Deepak called Felix.

"Stay tuned."

Felix was in the front chair when the CI suggested.

"Since when has Father been missing?"

"He took the car at nine o'clock. He did not say where. "

"Didn't you ask?"

"No. Ask and he will get angry. But the Morning Prayer will have Father anyway. That's it. Consulting will begin at 8 p.m. Today that routine went wrong. Will be trying on the phone from 6 am. But the phone is switched off. "

"Did you call all the places you could go?"

"Yes, He usually goes to the Math in Kolancherry and the Orphanage in Chottanikkara. Has not got there. "

When Felix stopped speaking, CI Mohandas told SI:

"Quickly contact the cyber cell and ask them to track Father's phone. Say you want all the call records of yesterday. "

"If it's a switched-off phone, tracking will not take place, sir."

"Take those call records. You know who called last. "

"Okay, sir. It will be available in half an hour. "

"Do one more thing. Need to find a car. It's a sedan car. Tell me the details, Felix. "

"It is a white i20 car. No. KL Seven 5345. "

"Report to all stations quickly. Ask to be notified if this car is found. "

“Okay, sir.”
ASI Pradeep contacted the control room.

SI spoke to the cyber cell.
The cyber cell woke up and worked because it was a sensational case.
The response came from the mobile company within half an hour.
The details came as a PDF file on CI's mobile.
“Take a printout of this. A total of 46 calls were received yesterday. Call everyone. Just start with the last number. Four people do this job quickly. I need to get the report within fifteen minutes. One thing should be called as if from the evangelical center. Let no one doubt. ”
The call began under the leadership of the assistant sub-inspectors.

Chapter 24

In the cabin, the CI, SI, and the panchayat president had a heated discussion.

"Father Gregorios Anastasio is a good man. No bad habits. He has created many fans with his miraculous healing. " Panchayat President Dominic said.

"Therefore, this case will be very sensational. It would be a big problem if the media got it. "

CI nodded.

"Yeah, the media make dirty stories. Now a Christian priest the media is well aware that there will be a good market if we stink. "

Dominic was overwhelmed.

Call reports came in shortly.

ASI Deepak said,

"Sir, except for three numbers, everything else is active. There is nothing suspicious. "

"Okay. Tap the address of those three numbers.

"There is an address in the call records."
"Hurry up."
The CI was rushed.
Then ASI James came up with a new piece of news.
"Sir, it is reported that Father's car crossed the Paliyekkara toll."
"Good. What time? "
"At seven-thirty in the morning."
"Okay. Then the focus was on the north. Can you tell me to do a highway CCTV search? "
"If you have gone to Iditarod, sir."
"Anyway, all toll plazas should be searched. Inform the control room quickly. "
The CI instructed.
Then his mobile rang.
Is the Commissioner.
The CI politely answered the Commissioner's questions.
"If there is no result within 12 hours, the investigation will go to the SP level. The DGP has intervened. "
"Look, sir, he's probably gone somewhere without saying a word. Father's car was reported at Paliyekkara toll plaza. The matter does not seem to be complicated. "

"Okay."
The commissioner hung up the phone.

CI was upset.
"We have to do something. I have reassured him that there is nothing wrong with that. .. Hello Jayaraman? "
"Sir ..."
"Bring all three addresses on the call list. No matter where you go, the headache will not go away without confirming it. "
"Sir, there is a list. Krishnakumar from Thiruvananthapuram one, Mallikabhavanam two, Peter, 12-234, Good Will Lane, Thripunithura, three Sebastian Kandathil Bungalow South Mazhuvannur. "
"Let that Thiruvananthapuram stay there. Chcck the other two now and leave each one directly. "
"Okay, sir."
SI Jayaraman left the cabin and left.

oooooo

ASI Deepak's bike came to a halt in front of the bungalow.
Deepak was in thc mufti.

He looked around to see that the gate was locked.

He saw a man coming on a bicycle on the road and stopped him.

"Hello dude, is there anyone in this house?"

"Was there?"

"The gate is locked."

"It's been two days since I last saw Sir Sebastian. His wife is here. Or there will be workers. Pappachan will see. "

"Who is Pappachan?"

"He is the servant of there."

"I do not see anyone here. Do you know his house? "

"I'm busy."

"I am a policeman. One thing to know. "

When he found out that it was from the police, the passerby agreed to show Pappachan's house.

He parked his bicycle on the side of the road and got on the back of Deepak's bike.

It was only half a kilometer from there to Pappachan's house.

Pappachan was at home.

When Pappachan found out that Deepak was from the police, he is in fear.

"I need the address of a mobile number."

Deepak said the number and address

"The address is correct sir, Sebastian, Kandathil Bungalow, South Mazhuvannur. The number is used by madam. "

"Madam?"

"Yes, Salome She is Sebastian's wife."

"Where are they?"

"Have you been to Bangalore? Yes, sir. "

"Call them on your phone ...?"

Pappachan immediately dialed the number and called.

"The Phone is switched off."

"Is that the problem?"

"But she used to call me in the morning. By the same number. "

"Then what did she say?"

"She said she was going to Bangalore."

"How long has it been since the phone rang."

When Deepak asked, Pappachan looked at the phone and told him when the call came.

"Sir, it's half-past eight." "

"No one is home right now, is there?"

"Sir is also from Bangalore. Maybe Salome will go there now. I know when I call in the morning. "
"Didn't she tell you then?"
"Yes sir. She did not even tell Katrina. "
"Who is that?"
"The cook in the bungalow."
"Do you know Father Gregorios Anastasios?"
"Who is that?"
"Didn't you come here?"
"I have not seen. What, sir? "
"He is an acquaintance of mine."
"Were you here yesterday?"
"There was. But on the farm and in the fields, the workers kept telling each other thing. "
"Salome?"
"She was at home. But I do not know if she went anywhere. Because I would move back and forth. How do I know if I'm out of that gap? "
"Okay. Thank you. "
Deepak said goodbye to Pappachan and left

Chapter 25

ASI Jayaraman got new news.
That information was an important turning point in the investigation.
The SI immediately informed CI Mohandas about it.
"We got the CCTV footage of the Paliyekkara toll plaza. Father's car was driven by a woman. "
"Woman?"
"Yes."
"Was Father in the car?"
"No. No one else. This woman was the only one in the car. They were driving the car. "
"Then where did Father go ... Is there something wrong with this ...?"
CI Mohandas stood up and walked like a crow.
He directed the SI in a hurry
"Ask them to take a picture of the woman from the CCTV footage."
SI called CPO Sooraj and told him about it.

"Freeze the video and print out a picture of the woman."
"Jayarama ...?"
The CI called
"What, sir?"
"Is that Felix there?"
"Looks like he went out for tea."
"Call him."
Jayaraman called Felix on the phone.
Felix arrived within ten minutes.

CI asked Felix:
"Did anyone come to see Father in particular yesterday?"
"There are visitors. You see forty or fifty people a day.
"Did something unusual happen?"
"If you ask me what is unusual ..?"
Felix is in consultation.
"Father's car has been cleared to cross the Paliyekkara toll. It was driven by a young woman. Father was not in the car."

"Lord.I hears something like this ... something is wrong sir ..."
Felix said excitedly.

By then CPO Sooraj had come to the cabin with a picture of the woman.

Jayaraman took it and handed it over to the CI.
CI showed Felix that picture
"Do you know this woman?"
Felix bought the picture and looked at it.
"No sir .... But I have seen them somewhere. I think this woman came there yesterday. Token not taken. Went straight to Father's room. Father argued and left. They then quarreled without stopping to pick up the token. "
"Isn't there CCTV?"
"Yes sir."
"Jayarama ... go to their office with Felix and look at the CCTV footage of yesterday."
"Okay sir ... but come on Felix."
Jayaraman also picked up Felix.

oooooo

At noon on the top of Mutharamala, a blanket of mist stood like white silk wrapped around a picture gallery.
In the cold, white smoke mingled with the mist.
Uttaswamy was chanting the mantra in front of the Homakunda with his body

completely naked. Waves of chanting filled the hut like a roar.

Anoop curled his tail in fear and moved to the corner of the verandah.

He was looking at someone ugly.

Fear rolled down his cheeks.

Uttamaswamy's right ear hearing the murmur.

"She is coming. It's time for his birth. "

"Om Karnapisachini Swaha ..."

Uttaswamy put a handful of mustard into Homakunda.

"Hunting dogs are after you.

"Order Swamini ..."

Uttaswamy stabbed the lemons with a broomstick and put them in the home kunda.

At that time, the jeep in which SI Jayaraman and Felix were traveling crashed into a Torres lorry. The incident took place at Mamalakkavala.

Both were seriously injured.

Both were taken to hospital.

The news came as a shock to CI Mohandas.

But got another piece of news.

Father's car was found abandoned.

Was found on National Highway 66 near Pachakil junction near Kozhikode. Nothing, in particular, could be seen inside the car.
Dog brought in the squad.
The police dog sniffed from the car and came to a stop at the nearest bus stop.

CI Mohandas who got the information guessed:
"The woman must have got on the bus. But I do not know where it may have gone. The problem is getting complicated. "
ASI Deepak is now in charge of SI. He had just gotten there from the hospital.
"Deepak, how are Jayaraman and Felix?"
"Seriously sir ..."
"That is very sad. Do one thing. The printout was in Jayaram's hands. Tell him to take another one. "
Deepak went outside the cabin.

But a few minutes later he came back disappointed and said
"Sir, it looks like that file has been deleted. Missing on computer. "

"It simply came to our notice then. Look at the video on my WhatsApp. "
CI looked at the WhatsApp video.
That too is missing.
"What a miracle? Where did that video go ... Do one thing, you cannot leave it. Call Toll Plaza. Tell me to send that video again. "
"Okay, sir."
Deepak contacted the control room.
But to no avail.
To everyone's surprise, the CCTV footage had disappeared.
The windows that the police were opening to Salome were closing one by one.
CI Mohandas slammed into the table in frustration.
The phone and files on the table were scattered on the floor.

Chapter 26

It was noon when Salome arrived at the Anthery junction.

A jeep is ready to go to Pulippara Falls.

There are only four passengers.

The driver looked at Salome as he approached the jeep.

She is fully pregnant.

"Hello lady, the road is difficult ... Is there anything wrong?"

"No dude...doesn't be afraid."

Salome said.

She is ready to face anything.

A full-term pregnancy occurs in just three days.

No one is to be believed.

I am already responsible for four more murders.

The only reason is that Uthaswamy is that damned man.

She cursed the moment she seemed to see him.

Lalitha, that astrologer is the cause of everything.

No matter what I told them, it was my perseverance that won. I do not know.

The jeep began to shake and move forward.
The driver kindly allowed her to sit in the front seat.
Then there was the gut-wrenching journey.
Salome often had abdominal pain.
The climb to Kodachadri Hill is easy.

When the jeep finally reached the Pulipara waterfall, Salome was paralyzed.
The driver asked:
"Hello lady is not in trouble, is she?"
"No, no problem."
"Is there no one with you ...?"
"Why ... why do people come to see this waterfall ... let's see if a woman can travel alone in our country ...?"
The driver then did not stop for further talk.

Salome walked with other tourists near the waterfall.
After staring at the waterfall cascading down the rocks for a moment, she slowly

began to walk down the sidewalk without anyone noticing.
The abdomen is beginning to ache well.
As if something inside was stirring.
The mind wants to see Utta Swamy as soon as possible.
No one can do anything but him.
Neither science nor medical science can answer this question.

Salome walked, imagining a one-way road through the woods.
The forest is getting wilder and wilder.
The roar of the waterfall and the noise of the tourists are gone.
Salome began to faint.
She sighed.
The legs are tired.
Thc abdomen hurts terribly.
She walked away with her skirt unbuttoned as the black long skirt continued to unravel.
But could not walk too far.
Salome fell to her knees.
The uterus water began to flow through the legs.
Salome screamed, unable to bear the pain in her abdomen.

That scream brought tremors all over the forest.

Uthaswamy stood up in the hut on the upper bank of the Mutharamala.
He dressed in red silk and took the magic wand in his hand and hurried out.
"Anoop come on ..."
Uthaswamy shouted.

Anoop, who was lying on the verandah, jumped down with Uthaswamy.
Then the two went down the hill at the speed of the storm.
Salome crawled through the darkness of the forest.
She rolled into a lush green forest.
The black skirt was soaked in blood.

The midday sun shone through the foliage of the big trees.
The howls of foxes rose all around.
She heard the sound of owls coming from somewhere.
The fog spread around like darkness.
Suddenly Salome screamed like a bamboo sheding.
Abdominal weight pushing down.
She pushed her legs in and out.

The foxes came closer, smelling the blood.
Their eyes shone wildly near Salome in the darkness.
An excruciating pain.
A wild cry.
The baby was born and fell to the ground.
Salome's consciousness was gone.
Meanwhile, Utta Swamy and Anoop were approaching.
He stood back as if he had gotten a hint of something.
He stopped Anoop who was barking with the howls of foxes.
An adorable baby opened its mouth and cried.
Within a short time, the foxes surrounded the mother and baby.
A fox bit its navel.
By then a great roar had shaken the forest.
A tiger jumped out of nowhere.
It drove the foxes away.
Then he bit the baby and walked away.
Anoop disagreed.
Uthaswamy stopped him.
The tiger turned for a moment and looked at Uttaswamy.

He bowed his head.
The tiger climbed into the forest and disappeared.
Uttaswamy took the unconscious Salome and put her on his shoulder.

Then walked fast.

Chapter 27

Salome regained consciousness.
Her body was wiped clean.
When she opened her eyes, Uttaswamy was sitting on the verandah drinking tea.
She stood up.
She hated him.
The baby's father is not this ugly old man.
She thought to herself.
"Didn't I tell you then that I was not the baby's father?"
Uthaswamy's sudden reply shocked her.
He is a great magician who reads the mind.
"Where is that baby?"
Salome asked.
"He is the son of the forest... a God ... and you are the mother of God."
"God? Isn't it the devil...?"
Salome asked angrily.
"He is the devil to those who see him as the devil. He is God to those who see him as God. "
Uttaswamy laughed.

"Do you want tea?"
"Yes"
Salome said.
He gave her a cup of tea.
She took it hot and drank it.
"Didn't all your wishes come true?"
The old man looked at her mockingly.
Salome looked at him with hatred.
Uthaswamy continued.
"Sebastian is his brother Williams, then your boyfriend Sandeep, and the poor magician Achen Gregorios. I was afraid of him. But it was lust that defeated him. The police will be looking for you soon.
"If the police catch me, I will catch you, ugly old man."
Salome quarreled.
Anoop sighed angrily at her.
"Don't bark, dog."
Salome responded.
Uthaswamy laughed out loud.
"He is not a dog."
"Then what? Are the human?"
"Dogs, foxes, humans, and worms are all just shirts, daughter. Some are tight, some are luxurious, some are torn ... The soul inside everything is true. He is the only one who survives time and death... Do you know who Anoop is..? "

"Tell me."

"My son ... He was a computer software engineer in Bangalore. Atheist. His human birth ended in an accident two years ago. Then my son was born as a dog and came to the Pulippara waterfall and waited for me. "

Uthaswamy's eyes filled with tears when he said that.

Anoop got up and licked his cheek.

Salome stared at it.

She drank the rest of the tea and got up from the floor.

"I need to take a shower."

Uthaswamy did not say anything.

He was staring at the sky, fondling memories.

Salome stared at him as she went.

She went to the back of the house, took off her clothes, drew water from the well, and washed her head.

"Water purifies everything."

She murmured.

There was a black mundu in the aya.

She takes it and wiped her body.

She did not cover her bare breasts.

She had a good appetite.

In a corner of the kitchen, she saw a pot of porridge.
She gulped down the porridge with salt and chilly.
She saw a green pumpkin in front of the stove.
She saw a dagger stuck in it.
She was also found bleeding from a stab wound to the pumpkin.
She pulled out the knife.
She wiped it on her clothes and slowly came to the door.
Uthaswamy is like that.
He is sitting meditatively with his feet down from the veranda and looking at the sky.
Salome was kneeling behind him.
She grabbed his head and put it on her chest as her nudity.
Uthaswamy looked up in disbelief.
Salome's hot breath hit his face.
His eyes were as numb as a dead fish.

Salome suddenly lowered the sharp knife to his chest with her right hand.
He was squirming like a chicken. Salome was holding a noose around his neck with her left hand.

But there was no expression on Uttaswamy's face.

The knife in Salome's hand rose again and again.

Her body was bathed in blood.

Naked breasts swarmed like two red eyes.

Seeing this, Anoop sighed and jumped.

Salome immediately picked up a large bucket full of water and hit Anoop on the head.

He was thrown into the yard.

Then he died.

Without Salome's capture, Uttaswamy also fell motionless into the yard.

Salome let out a sigh.

She spread her fingers and counted

"Six murders ..."

She took a shower again.

Dressed in red silk.

Then he opened the prayer room and went inside and closed the door.

ooooooo

10.30 pm _

Kochi City Police Commissioner Jagannath Sharma's office is busy holding discussions. A group of police officers is attending the meeting.

The commissioner said,

"No matter how much we hide the disappearance of Father Gregorios Anastasio in a mysterious situation, the media will make it sensational news. We have even received a call from the office of the Leader of the Opposition in Delhi. We need to find out where he is as soon as possible. We do not know whether he is alive or dead. It is now forty-eight hours since he went missing. The only evidence we have is that a woman was involved in his disappearance. From the video footage of CCTV footage of a bakery where the car was found, it is clear that the woman was fully pregnant. Video footage of the lost toll plaza was also recovered. CCTV footage of Father's evangelical center was also examined. The young woman who broke up with him that day was the same. The next step in front of us is to identify this woman. ACP Raveendran is in charge of investigating this case. "

ACP Raveendran, who was sitting in the front seat, stood up and saluted.

"Sir ..."

"Ravi is a respectful investigating officer of the Kerala Police in many criminal investigations. Get rid of this case as soon as you can. "

"Of course sir."

ACP Raveendran said confidently.

It was after midnight when the meeting ended.

In the middle of the night, one or two passers-by who had passed the second show from Kolencherry Pan Mall saw two figures indistinctly in the dark in front of the gate of the bungalow.

One is an old man and one is a dog.